In the
Small, Small Pond

For David, still the one.

Henry Holt and Company, LLC, *Publishers since 1866*
175 Fifth Avenue, New York, New York 10010
www.henryholtchildrensbooks.com

Henry Holt® is a registered trademark
of Henry Holt and Company, LLC.
Copyright © 1993 by Denise Fleming. All rights reserved.
Distributed in Canada by H. B. Fenn and Company Ltd.

Library of Congress Cataloging-in-Publication Data
Fleming, Denise. In the small, small pond / Denise Fleming.
Summary: Illustrations and rhyming text describe the activities of
animals living in and near a small pond as spring progresses to
autumn. [1. Pond animals—Fiction. 2. Stories in rhyme.]
I. Title. PZ8.3.F6378lm 1993 [E]—dc20 92-25770

ISBN-13: 978-0-8050-2264-3 / ISBN-10: 0-8050-2264-3 (hardcover)
25 24 23 22 21 20 19 18
ISBN-13: 978-0-8050-5983-0 / ISBN-10: 0-8050-5983-0 (paperback)
25 24 23 22 21 20 19 18 17
First published in hardcover in 1993 by Henry Holt and Company
First paperback edition, 1998
Printed in the United States of America on acid-free paper. ∞

In the
Small, Small Pond

Denise Fleming

Henry Holt and Company • New York

In the small, small

wiggle, jiggle,

tadpoles

wriggle

wings quiver

drowse, doze,

herons plunge

minnows scatter

circle, swirl,

whirligigs   twirl

sweep, swoop,

claws crack

dabble,

dip,

splish,
splash,
paws flash

pile,
pack,

muskrats
stack.

Chill breeze,

winter freeze...

cold night,

sleep tight,

small, small

pond.